Matter Comes In All Shapes

by Amy S. Hansen

Science Content Editor:
Kristi Lew

www.rourkepublishing.com

Science content editor: Kristi Lew

A former high school teacher with a background in biochemistry and more than 10 years of experience in cytogenetic laboratories, Kristi Lew specializes in taking complex scientific information and making it fun and interesting for scientists and non-scientists alike. She is the author of more than 20 science books for children and teachers.

www.rourkepublishing.com

Photo credits: Cover © Danylchenko Iaroslav, Lucie Lang, Maria Dryfhout; Cover logo frog © Eric Pohl, test tube © Sergey Lazarev; Page 5 © Werner Heiber; Page 7 © tacar; Page 9 © Jozsef Szasz-Fabian; Page 10 © K13 ART; Page 11 © Artistic Endeavor; Page 13 © matka_Wariatka; Page 15 © GraÃ§a Victoria; Page 16/17 © Alex Staroseltsev; Page 19 © Svetlana Larina; Page 20 © James Hoenstine; Page 21 © Thomas M Perkins

Editor: Kelli Hicks

Cover and page design by Nicola Stratford, bdpublishing.com

Library of Congress Cataloging-in-Publication Data

Hansen, Amy.
 Matter comes in all shapes / Amy S. Hansen.
    p. cm. -- (My science library)
 Includes bibliographical references and index.
 ISBN 978-1-61741-739-9 (Hard cover) (alk. paper)
 ISBN 978-1-61741-941-6 (Soft cover)
 1. Matter--Properties--Juvenile literature. 2. Matter--Constitution--Juvenile literature. I. Title.
 QC173.16.H36 2012
 530--dc22
                            2011003874

Rourke Publishing
Printed in the United States of America,
North Mankato, Minnesota
060711
060711CL

www.rourkepublishing.com - rourke@rourkepublishing.com
Post Office Box 643328 Vero Beach, Florida 32964

Table of Contents

What Is Matter?

Pour milk to make cookie dough. The milk is made of **matter**. Touch the bowl. The bowl is made of matter. Smell the cookies baking. It is matter you smell.

Eggs are made of matter, too.

Matter is everything that has **mass** and takes up space.

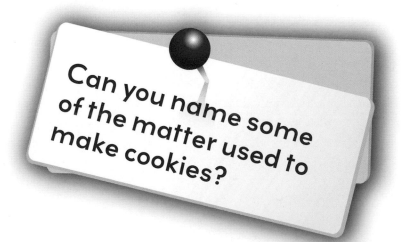

Can you name some of the matter used to make cookies?

Is All Matter the Same?

Matter can be a **liquid**, such as milk. It has mass and takes up space.

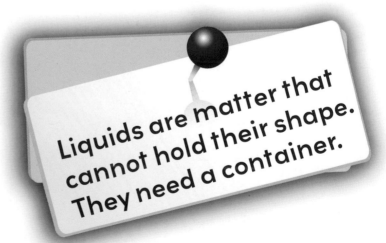

Liquids are matter that cannot hold their shape. They need a container.

Matter can be a **solid**, such as the bowl. It has mass and takes up space.

Matter can be a **gas**, such as air. The smell of the cookies is part of the air, a mixture of gases. It has mass and takes up space.

mmmm!

How do you know that gas takes up space? Blow into a balloon three times. Your breath is made of air. Now feel the balloon. That is how much space three breaths of air take up.

The balloon keeps the air from spreading out. Gases expand to fill the space.

Is your chair made of matter? Can you feel it? Does it take up space and have mass? Yes, your chair is made of matter.

A chair is a solid. Solids hold their shape.

What about water for washing? Does the water take up space and have mass? Yes, the water is made of matter.

What Isn't Matter?

What isn't made of matter? The light coming in your window is not matter. It is **energy**. Energy does not have mass or take up space.

19

Is Your Cookie Matter?

Now it is time to eat the cookie. You pick it up and feel it has mass. Is the cookie made of matter?

SHOW What You Know

1. Can you think of a liquid other than milk or water? Is that liquid made of matter?

2. How can you use a balloon to show gas taking up space?

3. What is not made of matter?

Glossary

energy (EN-ur-jee): the ability to do work; forms of energy include light or heat

gas (GAS): a substance that spreads out to fill the space available and is often invisible

liquid (LIK-wid): a substance that pours easily

mass (MASS): the amount of matter an object has, usually measured in grams or pounds

matter (MAT-ur): something that has mass and takes up space

solid (SAH-lid): an object that can hold its shape and is not a liquid or a gas

Index

Websites

www.kids-science-experiments.comwww.
www.exploratorium.edu/cooking/index.html
www.chem4kids.com

About the Author

Amy S. Hansen is a science writer living in the Washington, D.C. area. She uses matter every day to feed cookies to her two cats and cat food to her two sons. Or is it the other way around?